Clip-Clop

Nicola Smee

Boxer Books

“Who wants a ride?”
asks Mr. Horse.

"Me, please,"
says Cat.

Clip-clop,

clippity-

clop...

"I want a ride, too,
please, Mr. Horse," says Dog.

"Up you get,"
says Mr. Horse.

Clip-clop,

clippity-

clop...

"What about me?
I want a ride, too,
please, Mr. Horse,"
says Pig.

"Up you get,"
says Mr. Horse.

Clip-clop,

clippity-

clop...

"Don't leave me behind!"
says Duck.

"Up you get," says Mr. Horse.

"Can you go a little faster,
Mr. Horse?"
ask Cat
and Dog
and Pig
and Duck.

"Of course I can," says Mr. Horse, "but make sure you hold on TIGHT!"

Clippity-clop.

Faster, faster!

Clippity-clop.

Faster, faster!

Clippity-cloppity,

clippity-cloppity.

“Whoa! Stop! We’re falling off!”

squeal Cat and Dog
and Pig and Duck.

Mr. Horse skids to a
HALT!

And Cat
and Dog
and Pig
and Duck

fly through the air...

... and land in a haystack.

Plop!
Plop!
Ploppity-

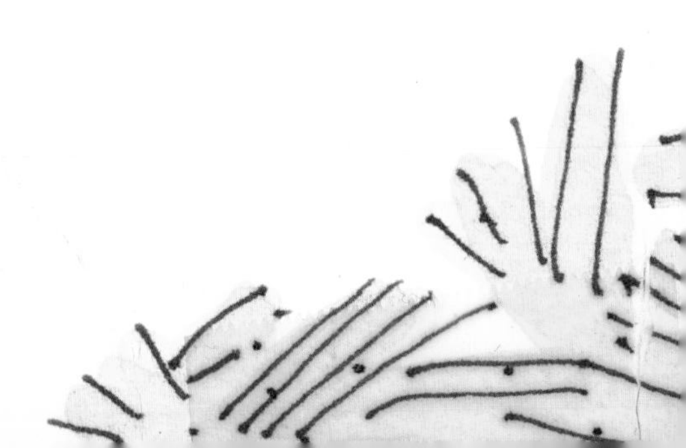

plop!

"Oh dear!
Oh dear!
Oh dearie me!"

says worried Mr. Horse.

“Ag

ain!"

cry Cat
and Dog
and Pig
and Duck.

"Up you get!" laughs Mr. Horse.

And Cat and Dog and Pig
and Duck go riding off again.

Clip-clop,

clippity-clop!

For CHROME HOOF
Nicola Smee

First American edition published in 2006
by Boxer Books Limited.

Distributed in the United States and Canada by
Sterling Publishing Co., Inc.
387 Park Avenue South, New York, NY 10016-8810

First published in Great Britain in 2006
by Boxer Books Limited.
www.boxerbooks.com

Library of Congress Cataloging-in-Publication Data available.

ISBN 10: 1-905417-09-8
ISBN 13: 978-1-905417-09-4

Printed in China